Greta
the Earth Fairy

Join the Rainbow Magic Reading Challenge!

Read the story and collect your fairy points to climb the

To Miranda, Richard, Greta and Emile

Special thanks to
Rachel Elliot

ORCHARD BOOKS

First published in Great Britain in 2020 by The Watts Publishing Group

1 3 5 7 9 10 8 6 4 2

© 2020 Rainbow Magic Limited.
© 2020 HIT Entertainment Limited.
Illustrations © Orchard Books 2020

The moral rights of the author and illustrator have been asserted.
All characters and events in this publication, other than those clearly in the public domain,
are fictitious and any resemblance to real persons, living or dead, is purely coincidental.
This publication is in no way endorsed or authorised, by Greta Thunberg and has no connection with
any organisation, or individual, connected with her.

A CIP catalogue record for this book is available from the British Library.

ISBN 978 1 40836 242 6

Printed and bound in Great Britain by Clays Ltd, Elcograf S.p.A

MIX
Paper from
responsible sources
FSC® C104740
www.fsc.org

The paper and board used in this book are made from wood from responsible sources

Orchard Books
An imprint of Hachette Children's Group
Part of The Watts Publishing Group Limited
Carmelite House, 50 Victoria Embankment, London EC4Y 0DZ

An Hachette UK Company
www.hachette.co.uk
www.hachettechildrens.co.uk

Greta
the Earth
Fairy

By Daisy Meadows

ORCHARD

www.rainbowmagicbooks.co.uk

Contents

Story One:
The Glittering Spoon

Story Two:

The Crystal Plug

Story Three:

The Sparkly Leaf Necklace

Jack Frost's Spell

I want glory, wealth and fame.
The human world should know my name!
I'll cause the planet lots of harm
And fill the people with alarm.

When seas are choked with plastic bags
And boys and girls are wearing rags,
Then hero Jack will save the Earth
And everyone will know my worth!

Story One
The Glittering Spoon

Chapter One
An Exciting Competition

"I'm so happy that it's half term and we get to spend the whole week together," said Rachel Walker.

She linked arms with her best friend, Kirsty Tate. They were walking along Tippington High Street towards the town hall. Kirsty was carrying the poster they had designed together for the Tippington eco competition.

"I'm glad they're going to announce the winner tomorrow," said Kirsty.

"I can't wait to find out who it is."

The town council had decided to remind people of all the things they could do to help the planet. Every child in Wetherbury had been invited to design a poster. The winning design would go up all over town.

At the town hall, there were queues of children going in and out. The air was filled with excited chatter. As the best friends ran up the steps, a girl with long brown hair waved to them.

"Hi, Rachel," she called. "Are you here to enter the competition?"

"Hi, Lara," replied Rachel. "Do

you remember my friend Kirsty
from Tippington? We're entering the
competition together."

They showed Lara their poster, and
then she unrolled hers. Rachel and Kirsty
gasped.

"Wow, that's really good," said Rachel.

"It's brilliant, Lara," said Kirsty. "You're a talented artist."

The poster was filled with pictures that showed things that people could do to every day to help the environment.

"Recycling, saving water, not using plastic, walking instead of driving, eating sustainable food . . . you've thought of everything," Kirsty said.

"I did it with my sister Isla," Lara explained.

"We did ours together too," said Rachel. "Working as a team made it even more fun."

"Good luck in the competition," said Lara with a smile.

"You too," said Rachel and Kirsty.

They went into the town hall where a

woman was collecting the posters. She already had a big pile.

"Another one for me?" she said, her eyes sparkling. "How wonderful. I can't wait to look at them all!"

Kirsty looked at her name badge.

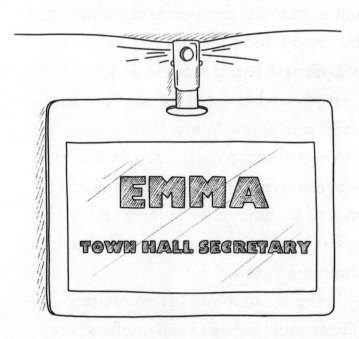

EMMA

TOWN HALL SECRETARY

"Thanks, Emma," she said. "Do you know when the winner will be announced?"

"Tomorrow," said Emma. "We want to get these posters up as soon as possible. We have to move fast to save the planet, and every little thing helps. The winner will put up the first poster right outside the town hall."

Sharing an excited smile, Rachel and Kirsty bounded down the steps . . . and stopped in shock. When they had gone into the town hall, the street had been neat and clean. But now there were piles of plastic bottles spilling into the road. Crisp and sweet packets littered the pavement.

"What is going on?" Rachel asked. "How could all this have happened in just a few minutes?"

They watched people walk past,

throwing their rubbish down. As well as
bottles, there were straws, spoons, bags,
packaging – all made of plastic. Rachel
and Kirsty made their way down the
street, wading through the litter. As they

passed a parked car, the owner got in
and turned on the radio. It was playing
the local news.

"…and finally, three of the nearest
beaches to Tippington have had to close,"
said the news presenter. "The amount
of plastic in the
water and on
the sand would
stop anyone from
swimming. No
more days on the
beach, folks!"

"He doesn't
sound upset
about it at all,"
said Kirsty,
leaning against
a nearby tree.

"It's as if he doesn't care about the planet being choked," said Rachel. "This doesn't make sense. Earlier, everyone was trying to do their bit for the environment. What's happened to them?"

"Jack Frost," said a tinkling voice from above.

The girls looked up and gasped. A tiny fairy was beckoning to them through the branches. Rachel and Kirsty didn't

hesitate. In a flash, they had climbed the tree and were sitting on a high branch. The leaves hid them from the street below.

"Thank you for coming up to talk

to me," said the little fairy in a solemn
voice. "I'm Greta the Earth Fairy, and
I desperately need your help."

Chapter Two
A Surprise in a Tree

Greta was wearing an anorak that was as yellow as a sunflower, and her brown hair hung over her shoulders in two long plaits. Her peached-coloured wings glimmered.

"It's great to meet you," said Kirsty.

"Are you here because of all the

plastic?" Rachel asked. "Do you know what's happening?"

"Yes, I do," said Greta, looking worried. "You see, it's my job to help people care about the environment and remember how to look after it. But Jack Frost has played a horrible trick on me. I'll show you what happened."

She waved her wand, and a knot hole opened up in the tree trunk. Pictures appeared inside, just like a film in a cinema. The girls saw Greta in a Fairyland forest, walking along in the dappled sunlight.

"I was enjoying the sunny morning and then I reached a pool that I had never seen before," the fairy explained. "I love wild swimming, so I decided to jump in."

In the tree cinema, Greta waved her

wand and changed into a swimming costume. She took a small cotton pouch from around her neck and set it on the ground beside her rucksack.

"What's that?" asked Kirsty.

"It's where I keep the three magical objects that help me," said Greta. "The glittering spoon motivates people to cut down on plastic, the crystal plug helps them to remember not to use too much water, and the sparkly leaf necklace inspires everyone to eat more vegetables and less meat and dairy. Inside that pouch is what we need to save the planet."

Rachel and Kirsty watched as Greta star-jumped into the pool. She swam into the middle, and then there was a squawking sound. Three goblins were standing on the bank, tossing the little pouch from one to the other.

"What are you doing?" Greta called out. "Give that back!"

"No way," one of the goblins yelled.
"We're just following orders. Jack Frost
wants this so that he can be king of the
world."

The goblins cackled with laughter, and
the picture faded.

"By the time I had swum out of the
pool, the goblins had vanished," Greta
told the girls. "Now Jack Frost has
my objects and the whole world is in
danger. I don't know what to do, but I
thought that you might help me. You're
Fairyland's best friends."

"Of course we'll help," Kirsty said at
once.

"Let's go straight to Jack Frost's castle,"
said Rachel.

Greta's smile lit up her face.

"I knew I could rely on you," she said.

She waved her wand, and a swirl of
sparkling fairy dust whooshed through
the leaves, making them shake and rustle.
The branches curved around the girls,
cradling them and lifting them higher.
They felt themselves shrinking to fairy
size, their gossamer wings unfurling. Then

the leaves fell away and Rachel and
Kirsty tumbled with them, transformed
into tiny fairies.

"Welcome back to Fairyland Rachel
and Kirsty!" said Greta.

Chapter Three
Secret Tunnels

The sky around them was grey, and thick flakes of snow kept bumping into their wings. Greta pulled a woolly hat out of her pocket and popped it on to her head. Then she waved her wand. Instantly, Rachel and Kirsty were wearing bobble hats and fleece-lined anoraks. They felt so much warmer.

"Look down there," said Greta, pointing
to the grim battlements of Jack Frost's
castle. "How are we going to get in?"

They flew lower and saw that the
drawbridge had been raised up. Every
window was barred, and the battlements
were empty. Kirsty bravely swooped
down and tried to open the secret
trapdoor entrance they had found before,
but it was locked. The fairies looked at
each other in dismay. They sank down to
the gardens behind the castle. Everything
was blanketed in a thick layer of snow.
The fairies perched on an icy tree
branch, and Greta buried her face in her
hands.

"Don't worry," said Rachel, putting
her arm around Greta. "We can work

this out together. We're a team. Isn't that right, Kirsty? Kirsty?"

But Kirsty didn't seem to be listening. She had tipped her head to one side and was sitting very still.

"Can you hear that?" she asked.

"What?" Rachel replied. "I can't hear anything."

"It's almost as if the tree is whispering," said Kirsty. "But it can't be, can it?"

"Oh yes, it can," said Greta in an excited voice. "Sometimes the trees tell me things because they know that I help to take care of them."

She pressed her ear to the chilly tree trunk and listened. Rachel and Kirsty waited, holding their breath. They saw Greta's sunshine-smile spread across her face.

"Thank goodness you were listening, Kirsty," she said. "The trees are going to help us! There is a maze of secret tunnels underneath the castle, and the trees know the way through."

She tapped her wand on the trunk and a fairy-sized door opened. Rachel felt hope and excitement bubble up inside her.

"Come on!" she said.

They swooped down the centre of the tree trunk and found themselves in a narrow tunnel.

"Which way?" asked Greta.

A tree root poked out of the soil and pointed along the tunnel like a finger.

"I think it's telling us to go right," said Kirsty.

Greta made her wand glow to give them a light, and they set off. As they flew along the passage, more tree roots pointed the way for them. The tunnel was damp and smelled of fresh earth. After turning down many forks and

bends, guided by the helpful trees, the
fairies reached a wooden door set into
the soil. A tree root tapped on it and then
disappeared into the tunnel wall.

"This must lead into the castle," said
Rachel.

"What if there's a goblin on the other

side?" Kirsty asked.

"We have to risk it," said Rachel in a determined voice. "Just think about all that plastic swirling in the sea and piling up on the pavements. The planet is depending on us."

Chapter Four
Jack Frost's Feast

Rachel turned the handle and the door creaked open. Slowly she peeped out, her heart hammering.

"It's OK," she said, relieved. "There's no one here."

They all flew out and looked around.

"I know this place," said Kirsty.
"We're in the dungeons. I remember
being trapped down here with Teri the
Trampolining Fairy."

"Oh my goodness," said Greta. "Let's
not get trapped today."

Rachel and Kirsty led the way out of
the dungeons. They went carefully, but
there were no goblins to be seen.

"Where is everyone?" asked Kirsty.

"I can hear something," said Rachel.

They all listened and heard a distant
rumble. As they followed the sound, it
grew louder, leading them towards it.
They passed the throne room which
stood empty. They passed the kitchen,
where dirty pots and pans were stacked
high. The noise was much louder now,
and the fairies could hear stamping feet

and squawking voices.

"Here," said Kirsty, stopping outside a large door.

The din was tremendous. Clamping their hands over their ears, the fairies pushed the door open and looked in.

"The whole of Goblin Grotto must be

here," said Rachel in astonishment.

The vast banqueting hall was packed with goblins. Some were eating at a huge table and others were leaning against the wall, scoffing handfuls of cakes, pies and sweets. The sound of stamping feet, squawking quarrels and scraping chairs

was deafening. At the head of the table, Jack Frost was roaring out orders at the top of his voice.

"Shut up, you pack of ninnies and nincompoops," he bellowed. "Listen to me, because I'm the only one around here with anything interesting to say."

The noise dropped, and Jack Frost stood up, holding a cup high in the air.

"That's a plastic cup," said Greta.

"Everyone has plastic cups," said Kirsty, gazing around.

"And plastic cutlery and straws," Rachel added, feeling confused. "Jack Frost doesn't seem to care about the environment, so why has he stolen your magical objects?"

"Today, we're celebrating the fact that I've beaten that goody-two-shoes Earth Fairy," Jack Frost announced. "Now I own those three magical objects, I can become famous all around the world."

One goblin's hand crept into the air.

"Yes, what do you want?" Jack Frost barked at him.

"How are those three things going to

make you famous?" the goblin asked.

"Because, you numbskull, human beings are starting to care about the planet," Jack Frost explained. "Without her magical objects, the Earth Fairy can't protect the planet. It'll turn into a stinky, littered mess. Then I'll use the objects to sort out the problems, and I'll be a hero. I'll be on the news and meet presidents and prime ministers, kings and queens. Every newspaper will want to write about me, and everyone will admire and respect me, me, ME!"

He hit the table with every "me", making all the plastic cups fall over.

"He doesn't care about the planet," said Kirsty. "He just cares about what people think of him."

"I'll save the planet," Jack Frost boasted.

"They'll probably make me king of the world."

"Please, your chilly iciness," said a goblin, stepping forward. "What are you going to do with the objects while you wait for the planet to get sick?"

Jack Frost beckoned him closer with a long, bony finger. He pulled three blue velvet pouches from inside his cloak. Each was marked with the initials J.F. in silver.

"Those must be my magical objects," said Greta with a gasp.

"Take this," Jack Frost said.

He handed a pouch to one goblin, and then pointed at two others. "You – and you – take these. Hide these pouches in places where the Earth Fairy would never think to look."

There was a loud crack and the goblins

disappeared in a flash of blue lightning.

The fairies exchanged a worried look.

Where could the goblins have been sent?

Chapter Five
Greedy Garden Goblin

In a daze, the fairies made their way out of the castle and back to the snowy trees.

"Jack Frost sent the goblins to places where I would never think to look," said Greta. "They must be places I would really dislike. Perhaps an airport guzzling up lots of fuel, or a city centre choked with car fumes?"

"How about a plastic factory?' Rachel suggested.

But Kirsty shook her head.

"None of those make sense," she said, thinking hard. "Jack Frost would expect Greta to think of those places. What if he has hidden the objects somewhere that she loves?"

"That's a brainwave," said Rachel. "Greta, where is your favourite place in the world?"

"That's easy," said Greta. "Home."

Rachel and Kirsty exchanged a knowing look.

"I bet Jack Frost would find it funny to hide your magical objects right under your nose," said Kirsty.

"Let's go and find out," said Greta.

"Follow me!"

The fairies left the castle gardens and zoomed towards the blue skies and green hills of Fairyland. Greta's toadstool house overlooked the sea, which sparkled in the

sunshine. Outside, a vegetable garden and an orchard nestled next to a little spring of fresh water. Vines and twisting roses were entwined over a table and chairs, lit by twinkling solar lights.

"What a beautiful place," said Rachel.

"Look," Kirsty cried. "There's a goblin in your garden!"

He was in the carrot patch, digging up the soil with his hands like a dog burying a bone. The fairies landed in front of him and he let out a shriek.

"You made me jump," he complained. "Go away, silly fairies. I'm busy."

"You have something that belongs to Greta," said Kirsty. "Please give it back to her."

The goblin shook his head so hard that his eyes wobbled.

"I bet you don't even know what's inside the pouch," said Rachel. "You poor thing. You had to leave the banquet early and you don't even know why. You must be hungry."

The goblin scowled. Then he tugged open the little velvet pouch he was carrying.

"A spoon?" he exclaimed. "What use is a spoon without any food?"

"That must be my glittering spoon," Greta whispered.

"Something to eat would be much more useful," said Kirsty. "How about a swap? Greta could give you some delicious food."

"Sweets?" asked the goblin, rubbing his tummy. "Crisps?"

Greta shook her head.

"The packets can't be recycled,"
she said. "How about something even
yummier?"

She waved her wand and a basket of
scrumptious food appeared. Pies and

muffins, fresh sandwiches, a bottle of
sparkling elderflower pop, strawberries,
blackberries . . . The goblin's tummy
rumbled loudly.

"Who needs a silly old spoon?" he said.
"I can eat with my hands."

He flung the pouch at Greta and
snatched up the basket. As he hurried
away, Greta pulled a dazzling spoon out
of the velvet pouch.

"Thank goodness," she said, beaming
with happiness. "Now I can get the
plastic problem under control."

The spoon glowed as it started to work
its magic. Greta turned to Rachel and
Kirsty.

"Thank you from the bottom of my
heart," she said. "Thanks to you, people
are remembering to cut down on how

much plastic they use again."

"We were glad to help," said Rachel. "And we won't stop until all your magical objects are back where they belong!"

Story Two
The Crystal Plug

Chapter Six
Water Worries

Rachel and Kirsty whirled around in a flurry of sparkling fairy dust. When it cleared, they were standing on the Tippington town hall steps.

"We're back to our usual size," said Kirsty, feeling a little dizzy.

"And Tippington High Street is back to

plastic free," said Rachel.

They gazed around. The piles of
plastic that had littered the streets
and pavements earlier had completely
disappeared. Rachel and Kirsty
exchanged a happy smile.

"Where is Greta?" asked Kirsty. "Did
she stay behind in Fairyland?"

"I'm here," said a
muffled voice.

Greta
peeped out
from under
Rachel's hair
and waved
at Kirsty.
"I hope
that we can
find my other

magical objects soon," she said. "But where should we look next?"

"Jack Frost hid the glittering spoon at your home," said Rachel. "Maybe he hid the other objects somewhere else you love. What are your favourite places?"

"I have so many favourites," said Greta. "I don't know how to tell which one he would have picked. What am I going to do?"

"Queen Titania always says that we should wait for magic to find us," said Kirsty.

"My dad is making a picnic for us," Rachel remembered with a rush of excitement. "We can all go. Maybe something will happen to give us a clue about Jack Frost's plans."

Greta tucked herself under Rachel's

hair again, and the girls hurried home.
As they passed a front garden, they heard
the pitter-patter of water drops. The girls
peeped over the fence.

"They've got a sprinkler watering their
grass," said Kirsty in surprise. "That's not
very eco-friendly."

"No, it's a big waste of water," said
Greta.

"Look, the house next door has got one
too," said Rachel. "And the next . . . and
the next."

Every house they passed had a
sprinkler on. It seemed as if everyone in
Tippington had forgotten about saving
water.

"Your picnic's ready, girls," called Mr
Walker as they walked in. "I'm just
washing up."

Rachel and Kirsty hurried into the kitchen. A picnic basket was waiting on the table, covered in a red checked cloth. Kirsty started to look at the food, but Rachel was staring at her dad. He was washing up with the tap running. Water was splashing everywhere and running down the drain.

"Dad, you always tell me to fill a bowl with water to wash up," she said.

"Do I?" said Mr Walker in an absent-minded voice. "Oh, I'm sure it doesn't really matter. A lot of fuss about nothing, I expect."

Rachel and Kirsty shared a worried glance. They had never heard Mr Walker talk like this before. He was usually eager to do everything he could to help the planet.

"This is because of the missing crystal plug," Greta whispered. "Without it, everyone will forget to be careful with water."

"We have to find a way to get it back," said Kirsty.

Rachel picked up the picnic basket.

"Let's go and enjoy our lunch," she said. "We can talk about what to do next while we eat."

At that moment, Mr Walker let out a cry of surprise.

"Goodness me, what's happened?" he exclaimed.

Chapter Seven
Grotto World

The gush of water from the tap had slowed down to a dribble. Instead of running clear, it was brown and gloopy.

"I've never seen that happen before," said Rachel. "Has the water run out?"

"That's impossible," said her dad. But he looked confused. Rachel beckoned to Kirsty.

"This must be to do with the crystal plug too," she said. "Let's have our picnic by Tippington Spring, where the freshest local water comes from. It's usually quiet up there, so we'll be able to talk to Greta in peace."

As they set off along the street, front doors kept opening. People called to their neighbours, looking confused.

"The water has stopped working!"

"Brown water is coming out of my taps."

"Where has all the water gone?"

Rachel and Kirsty hurried towards the woods and climbed over a little stile. As soon as they were sure that there was no one else around, Greta fluttered out.

"There's the spring," she called out.

"I love this place. Oh, but it's not
working."

The little spring was usually bubbling
and gurgling. But today there was no
water coming out of the ground.

"I can't understand it," said Greta.
"The crystal plug helps people to
remember to save water, but it shouldn't

make it run out."

The girls put down the basket. Before they could unwrap their sandwiches, they heard a strange noise.

"What was that?" asked Kirsty.

"It sounded like a cackle," said Rachel. Suddenly, two goblins darted out of

the woods and started to dance around the spring. They were squawking with laughter, and one of them was carrying a blue velvet pouch.

"We did it, we did it, the water's gone away!" they sang.

Rachel jumped to her feet, and the taller goblin yelled in surprise.

"Yikes!" he cried. "It's those interfering humans that Jack Frost can't stand. Clear off, you. Shoo!"

"You've got something that doesn't belong to you," said Kirsty, pointing at the velvet pouch.

"None of your business," snapped the smaller goblin.

He stuck out his tongue and blew a loud, wet raspberry at them all.

"Let's go to Goblin Grotto," said the

taller goblin. "It's more fun there."

They darted off, and Rachel shared a confused look with Kirsty.

"I've never heard a goblin call Goblin Grotto 'fun' before," said Kirsty.

"Let's follow them there," said Rachel. "We have to get that pouch."

Greta spun into the air, twirling her wand above her head. A cascade of glittering fairy dust sprinkled down on to the girls. At once, they shrank to fairy size. Tiny wings lifted them into the air, shimmering with rainbow colours.

They blinked, and they were fluttering high above the goblin village. From a thick cloud above them, a vast waterfall was pouring down into a huge barrel in the central square. From there, it was flowing down brightly coloured pipes

that snaked all around the village. The
fairies followed the pipes with their
eyes. Some of the water was filling up
swimming pools and one had frozen into

an ice rink. Other pipes led to water balloons, pedalo ponds, wishing fountains and slaloms. A huge sign with blue flashing lights arched over the village

spelling out *Grotto World*.

"Oh my goodness," said Kirsty. "The whole goblin village has turned into a water park!"

Chapter Eight
Water Snakes

There were open-air swimming pools on
every street corner. Water slides spiralled
down from the roofs of the goblin huts,
twisting through the streets and landing
in the pools.

"The goblins look happy," said Rachel.
Everywhere, grinning goblins were

leaping into pools and whooshing down water slides.

"Jack Frost must have stolen the human water supply and sent it all to the goblin village," said Greta with a groan. "Look – they're not wasting a drop. Everything is being used."

"It does look like amazing fun," said Rachel.

"The goblins will never agree to give up all of this," said Kirsty.

"Then we have to think of something clever," said Rachel. "There must be a way to get the water back to the human world."

"That's it!" cried Kirsty, twirling around in mid-air. "If Jack Frost found a way to send the water to Goblin Grotto, maybe we can do the same thing."

"Can you send it back?" Rachel asked Greta.

Greta bit her lip.

"Without my magical objects, I don't think I'll be able to send this water all the way back to the human world," she said.

"Then let's send it to the Fairyland Palace," said Kirsty. "If you can get it to the queen, I'm sure she'll know what to do."

"Great idea," said Greta, her face brightening. "Queen Titania is always kind and helpful."

The happy squeals of goblins filled the air as the fairies flew closer to the village.

"Luckily they're enjoying themselves so much, no one's looking out for fairies," said Rachel with a smile. "How are you going to do it, Greta?"

Greta held up her wand and spoke.

"Pipes of orange, red and gold,
Turn and spiral, bend and fold.
Pipes of yellow, blue and green,
Take your water to the queen!"

For a moment, nothing happened.

"Perhaps my magic isn't strong enough while Jack Frost still has two of my objects," said Greta.

"Wait, look," said Kirsty, pointing at a

red pipe that was leading to a rooftop swimming pool. It gave a little shiver and then rose into the air.

"It looks just like a snake," said Rachel, clapping her hands. "Well done, Greta!"

The goblins started to cry out as more of the colourful pipes pulled away, rising up towards the fairies.

"Look up there!"

"It's those annoying little fairies!"

"Throw snowballs at them!"

"Send them away!"

"I think it's time to go," said Kirsty, dodging a flying snowball.

Greta flicked her wand, but the snake-like pipes stayed where they were, swaying slightly in the icy breeze.

"I can't move them," she cried. "They're stuck!"

"Try again," said Kirsty, putting her arm around Greta. "I know you can do it."

Chapter Nine
A Super Helping Hand

The second time Greta flicked her wand, the pipes followed her as she flew away. Rachel and Kirsty stayed by her side, and the goblins' shouts faded into the distance. But they went more slowly than Rachel and Kirsty were used to flying. The pipes were full of water, and heavy.

"Oh, thank goodness," said Greta, looking down. "We've left the snow behind."

Green hills dotted with toadstool houses rolled ahead of them.

"The pipes are going to have to wind around the houses," said Rachel.

"I'm not sure my magic is strong

enough," said Greta, looking worried.

"I recognise this place," Kirsty said,
looking around. In the distance, she saw
a tall silver tower, sparkling in the
sunshine. "Rachel, do you remember?
That's where Samira the Superhero
Fairy lives."

"We had a wonderful adventure with
her," said Rachel.

"Jumping jellyfish," said a friendly voice.
"It looks as if it's time for another one."

A fairy wearing a suit of purple and
gold zoomed in front of them, did a
somersault and hovered with her hands
on her hips.

"Samira!" cried Rachel and Kirsty in
delight.

"I heard you talking about me with
my super hearing," said Samira. "I had to

come and say hello."

Quickly, the fairies explained what had happened.

"Now I need a little extra magic to get the pipes all the way to the palace," Greta explained. "It's taken me a long time to get them this far."

"A little extra magic coming up," said Samira, winking at Greta.

Kirsty glanced back towards Goblin Grotto and gasped. A rain cloud was speeding towards them, crackling with lightning.

"Oh my goodness," she said. "Samira, you're going to have to be quick. I can see Jack Frost riding on that storm cloud behind us!"

The Superhero Fairy darted ahead
of them, and the colourful pipes twined
together like ribbons and followed her.
They wound around toadstool houses
and zigzagged through forests and
orchards. Rachel and Kirsty flew side

by side with Greta.

"He's getting closer," called Kirsty, glancing over her shoulder. "Hurry!"

The Fairyland Palace was glittering up ahead. As the fairies reached the entrance, so did Jack Frost. He jumped off the rain cloud. A goblin was sitting on it, holding the blue velvet pouch in his bony fingers.

"Well, you silly little fairy," said Jack Frost with a smirk. "You can drag these pipes all around Fairyland as much as you like. But I have this pouch, so you can't send the water back to the

human world."

Rachel and Kirsty stepped in front of the pipes, which were tying themselves up in bows.

"The water in these pipes belongs in the human world," said Kirsty.

"Humans don't care about it," said Jack Frost. "They've been wasting the water, so I brought it here. I knew my goblins would look after it."

"That's not true," said Greta. "The humans only stopped caring about water when you stole the crystal plug."

Jack Frost sniggered, and the goblin on the cloud squawked with laughter. Rachel watched him playing with the pouch, weaving it between his fingers as he listened to Jack Frost.

"I'll be the king of the world when I

fix this mess," Jack Frost boasted.

"But you made the mess," cried Kirsty. "You're not being fair."

"I don't care about being fair, you ninny," said Jack Frost.

At this, the goblin laughed even harder, rolling around and clutching his tummy. As Rachel watched, he actually rolled

off the cloud and lay on the ground,
cackling. Then Rachel felt her heart leap
with excitement. The goblin had dropped
the pouch on the cloud – and he hadn't
noticed.

Chapter Ten
A Plug and a Prisoner

As Greta, Kirsty and Samira tried to
reason with Jack Frost, Rachel edged
towards the cloud. Could she reach it
before the goblin noticed? The goblin sat
up and started to turn back to the cloud.
Rachel threw herself towards it, reaching
out for the pouch.

"No, stop!" squeaked the goblin.

Jack Frost whirled around and yelled. Blue lightning crackled from his wand, and the cloud shot into the air.

"Rachel!" cried Kirsty.

Rachel tried to fly back down, but the puffy grey cloud held her wings like a magnet.

"Naughty little fairy," Jack Frost sang out, wagging one long finger at her. "You won't get the better of me, you know."

"Let me go," Rachel exclaimed, trying to pull her wings free.

"Promise to give me back my pouch and then I will think about it," said Jack Frost.

"It's not yours," Rachel said.

She looked at Kirsty and tilted her head a little. The best friends knew each other so well that they could often understand each other without words. Kirsty guessed that Rachel was about to throw the pouch to her. She fluttered away from Jack Frost.

"Catch!" Rachel called out.

She threw the pouch to Kirsty as hard as she could. It was a good throw. Kirsty leapt into the air and caught it, wrapping her body around it tightly.

"Excellent catch," Rachel cheered.

"Give that back!" howled Jack Frost.

Kirsty shook her head and handed
the pouch to Greta, who opened it. A
glimmering plug fell into her open hand.

"The crystal plug!" she whispered,
smiling. "Now I can put everything
right."

With a wave of her wand, the coloured

pipes vanished from in front of the palace.
Rachel and Kirsty clapped their hands.

"Does that mean that people have
water again?" Kirsty asked.

Greta nodded happily.

"Everything will be back to normal
when I send you home," she said.

"You blithering fool!" Jack Frost
screeched at the goblin. "Nincompoop!"

He pointed his wand at the cloud,
and there was a flash of blue lightning.
Instantly, the cloud sped away towards
the ice castle, with Rachel still stuck to it.
Kirsty stared at Jack Frost in shock.

"Bring her back!" she exclaimed.

"Hand over my pouch first," he
retorted.

At that moment, the palace entrance
opened and everyone turned to stare.

Queen Titania was standing in the doorway. Her expression was extremely stern.

"Jack Frost, you must return Rachel at once," she said. "You have lost your

temper and made a foolish choice, but
I know that you have goodness in you."

Jack Frost grabbed the goblin's wrist
and snarled at them all.

"That fairy is my prisoner," he shouted.
"And you will never get her back!"

There was a bright blue flash, and Jack
Frost and the goblin disappeared. Greta

and Kirsty exchanged a horrified glance.

"It's wonderful that we've got the crystal plug back," said Kirsty. "But how are we going to save Rachel?"

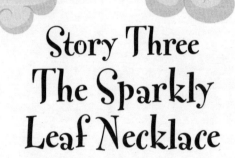

Story Three
The Sparkly
Leaf Necklace

Chapter Eleven
The Goblins' Captive

The cloud zoomed towards the Ice
Castle and headed straight for an open
window at the top of one of the towers.
It swooped in and tipped Rachel on to
the floor.

"Ouch," she said, fluttering to her feet.

"A prisoner!" squawked a voice behind

her. "A prisoner at last!"

Rachel whirled around. Two goblins were jumping up and down in excitement. There was a large cage behind them.

"You have to go in there," said the shorter goblin.

Rachel put her hands on her hips.

"Why should I?" she asked.

The goblins exchanged alarmed looks and did some fierce whispering. Then the taller one spoke.

"Er . . . Jack Frost said that if he ever sent a cloud in here with a fairy on it, we had to lock them in the cage and wait for him."

"That's terrible," said Rachel. "How many fairies have you locked in here?"

The goblins started whispering again,

then arguing and counting on their fingers. Rachel crossed her arms and waited.

"Er . . . none," said the shorter goblin. "You're our first prisoner. So go in."

"I shan't," said Rachel.

The goblins looked even more alarmed.

At that moment, there was a bright blue flash and Jack Frost appeared in the middle of the room, holding a goblin by the wrist. He glared at Rachel.

"Into the cage!" he hissed.

There was no way to argue. Rachel obeyed, and the door clanged shut.

"You will be guarded day and night," said Jack Frost. "My guards will watch you every second. They will not sleep or eat until my trap has worked."

The goblin guards stared at him in dismay.

"What trap?" Rachel asked.

Jack Frost gave an unpleasant smile. He pointed to the open window.

"Your pesky friends will try to rescue you," he said. "I'll lock every door and window in the place except this one. The candlelight and the open window will draw them in, and my guards will be waiting. Soon, you will all be my prisoners."

Rachel frowned. If her rescuers were captured, they could be trapped inside the Ice Castle for ever.

"Well, I just won't allow that to happen," she said to herself.

Jack Frost took a blue velvet pouch from his cloak and gave it to the guards.

113

"This is what the fairies want," he said. "Don't you dare let them get it. This is going to make me the king of the world."

He swept out, pulling the unlucky goblin who had lost the crystal plug with him. Rachel looked at her goblin guards. Somehow, she had to get out of the cage and get the last magical object away from them.

"Aren't you going to look and see what it is you're guarding?" she asked.

The goblins stuck their tongues out at her. Then they looked at each other.

"It can't do any harm to take a peek," said the taller one.

He pulled the pouch open and pulled out a gorgeous necklace with a leaf-shaped pendant. It glimmered in the candlelight.

"Greta's sparkly leaf necklace," Rachel murmured. "It's so beautiful."

"So how is this going to make Jack Frost the king of the world?" asked the smaller goblin.

"Don't be an idiot," said the taller one. "It's probably really valuable."

"No, it's magic," said the smaller one. "Maybe it turns into a crown when you put it on your head."

He jammed it on to his bony head, and the leaf dangled over his right ear.

Rachel couldn't help giggling.

"It's nothing to do with kings or crowns," she said. "It helps everyone remember to eat more vegetables and less meat or dairy. It's better for the planet."

"That's stupid," said the smaller goblin. "What has food got to do with the planet?"

"Animal farming needs farmland," Rachel explained. "Forests are being cut down to make room, and that hurts the planet. And animal farming makes greenhouse gases. They hurt the planet too."

"Do you mean that the humans are hurting their own world by eating the wrong things?" asked the taller goblin. "Ha ha! Hee hee! Silly humans!"

Cackling with laughter, the goblins shoved the necklace roughly into its pouch. The taller goblin stuffed it into his pocket.

"I have to get out," Rachel said to herself. "And I have to get that necklace!"

Chapter Twelve
Kirsty's Plan

After Jack Frost vanished from in front of the Fairyland Palace, Kirsty had turned to Queen Titania and curtseyed.

"I have to rescue Rachel, Your Majesty," she said in a determined voice. "May I go straight away?"

"Yes, of course," said the queen. "There

is no time to lose."

"I'll go with her," said Greta, tucking the crystal plug into the cotton pouch around her neck. "Now that two of my magical objects are safe again, I feel much stronger."

Samira suddenly tilted her head to one side as if she had heard something.

"I'm afraid I can't come," she said. "There's a problem with a helicopter in the human world and that's a job for a superhero."

"It's OK," said Kirsty, hugging her. "Greta and I will find Rachel. Thank you for your help."

"You're very brave," said Samira. "Good luck, both of you."

She gave them a super-fast hug and then zoomed up into the sky in a flash of

gold and purple. Kirsty turned to Greta.

"We have to get into the castle to search for Rachel," she said. "That means getting past the goblins, and I've had an idea. Can you use your magic to disguise us? If they thought that we were selling something they want, they might let us in."

"Of course," said Greta. "But what do

the goblins want?"

"A new water park," said Kirsty. "They were upset when we took the water pipes away from Goblin Grotto. If they thought that they could have a water park again, they might let us in. Then we could slip away from them and search the castle for Rachel."

Greta nodded and waved her wand. A ribbon of sparkling fairy dust wound around them both. Kirsty looked down and saw that her normal clothes had been replaced by a blue striped suit. Greta's raincoat had vanished too, and she was wearing a yellow striped suit.

"Good luck," said Queen Titania. "I will watch over you from my Seeing Pool."

Kirsty and Greta fluttered into the sky

and set off for the Ice Castle.

By the time they reached Jack Frost's home, it was night. A single light was burning at a high window.

It was the room where Rachel was

locked up, but Kirsty and Greta did not know that. The fairies landed behind some trees and tucked their wings out of sight. Greta's magic produced matching hard hats on their heads. Then Kirsty led the way to the main entrance.

"My heart is thumping like mad," she whispered to Greta. "I hope this works."

The door opened and a goblin squinted at them.

"What do you want?" he snapped. "We're busy."

Kirsty puffed up her chest, as she had seen goblins do when they felt clever and important.

"We want to help you," she said in a loud voice. "We are water park sellers, and we heard that some pesky fairies took away your Grotto World water

park. Would you like to buy a brand-new one?"

The goblin's eyes grew big and he pulled open the door.

"A new water park!" he squawked. "That would be brilliant!"

More goblins swarmed towards them
as they walked into the courtyard, all
shouting about what they wanted.

"More slides!"

"A hot tub!"

"Take them to Jack Frost!"

Chapter Thirteen
Searching the Castle

The fairies were led along dark, dripping corridors by the shouting goblins. The crowd grew bigger every moment. By the time they burst into the throne room, the noise was deafening. Jack Frost sprang up from his throne in surprise.

"Who are you?" he barked.

"They're selling water parks," one goblin explained.

"Can we have one?" said another. "Please?"

"Pretty please with a cherry on top?" said another.

"Yuck, cherries," said a third, shoving him. "Pretty please with a slime ball on top."

"We'll never do anything wrong ever again," called a goblin at the back of the crowd.

"Silence!" Jack Frost roared. "Why should I get you a new water park when you lost the last one?"

"It wasn't our fault," wailed one of the goblins. "It was those rotten fairies."

"You spoiled my plans," said Jack Frost. "Get out, the lot of you!"

Kirsty and Greta exchanged a worried glance.

"Wait," said Kirsty, stepping forward. "If you don't like the idea of a new Grotto World, how about a water park right here at the Ice Castle? It's the perfect spot. You could have helter-skelters winding around the towers and slides

coming down from the windows. You
could even have a hot tub in the garden."

Jack Frost stared at her.

"Go on," he said. "Tell me more."

"You could have fairground rides and
little boats on a lake," said Rachel. "How
about a swimming pool with a wave
machine?"

"What about inside?" said Jack Frost
greedily. "What could I have inside?"

Kirsty thought quickly. To be able to
find Rachel, they had to get away from
Jack Frost.

"We need to look around your castle
to see what we could fit in," she said. "Is
that OK?"

"Go on then," said Jack Frost, waving
his bony hand. "But hurry up, and
remember, this has to be the biggest and

best water park ever. I want everyone to be jealous of me."

Kirsty and Rachel dashed through the castle on foot. They didn't dare to use their wings in case a goblin saw them. They ran up and downstairs, along halls and corridors, and in and out of rooms. But there was no sign of their friend.

"There is one more tower to search,"

said Kirsty. "She must be in there."

They reached the spiral staircase of the tower and peered up.

"Rachel?" called Kirsty in a careful voice. "Are you there?"

"SPIES!" yelled a voice behind them.

They whirled around. Jack Frost was glaring at them.

"I came to see what was taking so long," he bellowed. "Who are you?"

Greta waved her

wand and their disguises melted away.

"Fairies," Jack Frost hissed. "I should have known a water park was too good to be true."

"We've come to take Rachel home," said Kirsty bravely. "Where is she?"

"She's my prisoner, just like you two," said Jack Frost. "Guards!"

"Rachel!" Greta cried out. "Rachel, where are you?"

Chapter Fourteen
Rachel's Escape

Meanwhile, Rachel had noticed one of the goblins give a huge yawn. An idea popped into her head and she started to hum. Then she began to sing. The candle flickered, and the other goblin yawned.

"It's working," Rachel told herself. "If I can get them to fall asleep, maybe

I can escape."

She sang lullaby after lullaby, and the goblins' eyes drooped, and dropped, and closed. At last, they both began to snore. The smaller goblin's hand fell open, and Rachel saw that he was holding the cage key.

Rachel pushed her hand through the

bars and stretched as far as she could reach. But it wasn't quite far enough. She glanced around. The goblins were not tidy, and there were lots of things lying on the floor around the cage. Springs from broken toys, empty sweet wrappers, jam jars, gloves missing their pairs . . . and a small candy cane.

"That's it," said Rachel.

The curved end of the cane easily hooked the key and pulled towards her. In a few seconds she had unlocked the cage. She was free!

Rachel leaned over the taller goblin, holding her breath. Very slowly, she pulled the pouch out of his pocket. Both goblins carried on snoring, and the pouch was hers. She darted towards the open window, ready to fly back to the

Fairyland Palace. But before she could leave, she heard loud voices. Someone was shouting her name.

Rachel flew to the door and flung it open.

"I'm here!" she shouted.

Rachel's goblin guards woke up and jumped to their feet.

"Catch her!" they yelled at each other.

Rachel zoomed down the spiral stairs, and the goblins chased her. At the bottom, Jack Frost charged towards the stairs. Rachel saw him at the last moment and darted sideways. *CRASH!* Jack Frost and the goblin guards ran into each other and landed in a tangle of arms and legs. Rachel flung her arms around Kirsty and Greta.

"I've got the sparkly leaf necklace," she

panted. "There's an open window at the top of the stairs. Hurry!"

While Jack Frost was tangled up with the goblins, the fairies flew over them and went up the spiral stairway.

"Stop!" Jack Frost screeched. "That necklace is mine!"

"It belongs to Greta," said Rachel in a firm voice.

She held the necklace out, and Jack Frost lunged for it.

Chapter Fifteen
Saving the World

The necklace was knocked out of
Rachel's hand. It glittered as it spun
through the air, and Jack Frost jumped
up to catch it. But Greta was faster. She
sprang up and caught the necklace in her
hand.

"Yes!" shouted Kirsty and Rachel

together. The necklace seemed to glow more brightly. Greta put it into the cotton pouch she wore around her neck.

"Now it's back where it belongs," she said. "I can already feel that things are being put right in the human world. People have started to remember to eat more vegetables and less meat and dairy."

Jack Frost shook his fist at the fairies.

"How am I going to be king of the world now?" he shouted.

"That's easy," said Greta. "You're not! The human world is safe again – from pollution, from plastic and from you."

The three fairies flew up to the room where Rachel had been kept and out through the window. Hovering above the cold battlements of the castle, they shared a hug in mid-air.

"You have both been amazing," said Greta. "Without you, the whole world would be in danger. Thank you for everything."

"We were glad to help," said Kirsty. "After all, the planet belongs to all of us, fairies and humans."

"It's everyone's job to keep it safe,"

added Rachel.

"Now you can relax and enjoy your picnic," said Greta. "Thank you again, and goodbye."

She flicked her wand, and a cloud of sparkles surrounded Rachel and Kirsty. They felt themselves spinning around, faster and faster, until Greta, the Ice Castle and all of Fairyland were one big blur. Then they landed with a gentle bump on a soft patch of grass. They were back in Tippington, and they were human again.

"What's that gurgling sound?" asked Kirsty, blinking.

"Tippington Spring," said Rachel. "Look, here's our picnic."

As usual, time had stood still in the human world while the girls were

in Fairyland. Sharing a smile, they
unpacked their picnic.

"This all looks so yummy," said Kirsty.
"Hey, have you noticed? It's meat and
dairy-free. Greta would be pleased!"

"I'm glad there are ways we can carry

on helping the planet," said Rachel,
patting the grass beside her.

Kirsty opened her sandwiches and
nodded.

"That's what the poster competition is
all about," she said. "And tomorrow we'll
find out who has won."

The next day, Rachel and Kirsty were
in a crowd of people in front of the town
hall. Emma, the town hall secretary, was
standing on the steps holding a rolled-up
poster.

"Thank you all for coming," she said.
"And thank you to all the children who
took part. One poster stood out above
all the others and was the clear winner.
It had so much detail about the things

we could be doing to help our beautiful planet. Well done, Lara and Isla!"

Beaming with happiness, the sisters went up to shake Emma's hand. Rachel and Kirsty cheered and clapped until their hands were sore.

"These wonderful posters will appear all over the town," said Emma. "They will be a great reminder to us all."

As Lara and Isla put their first poster up on the town hall noticeboard, Kirsty glanced at her best friend.

"Are you disappointed that we didn't win?" asked Kirsty.

Rachel shook her head.

"Not at all," she said. "I feel really lucky. We've had another amazing fairy adventure and we helped the planet. Although being taken prisoner was a bit scary!"

"I'm glad that Lara and Isla's poster won too," Kirsty said. "It shows people that everyone can help and little things can make a big difference – even without fairy magic!"

The End

Now it's time for Kirsty and
Rachel to help ...

Jacinda the Peace Fairy

Read on for a sneak peek ...

"What's the weather like?" asked Rachel
Walker, bouncing out of bed and darting
to the window. "Oh, I hope it's sunny."

She flung open her curtains and smiled.
Sunlight streamed into the room and her
best friend, Kirsty Tate, sat up in bed.

"Your wish is granted," she said,
laughing. "I wonder if the Weather Fairies
know that today is special."

Rachel and Kirsty had a wonderful
secret. They had learned that fairy magic
helped the human world every day,
even though most people never knew

it. Even better, they had made friends with the fairies and shared some exciting adventures with them.

"I don't suppose we'll see any magic today," said Rachel, pulling on a flowery dress. "It's all about ordinary hard work and people caring for each other."

Rachel's mother had been working on a special project. There was a patch of land in the middle of Tippington town that had been empty for as long as anyone could remember. For years, people had argued about how to use it. There had been many ideas and lots of squabbling. But at last, everyone had agreed on the perfect answer: a peace garden. After months of hard work, the opening ceremony was today.

"It's such a cool project," said Kirsty

as she got up and made her bed. "Were there lots of volunteers?"

"Dozens," said Rachel. "Everyone in the community wanted to be part of it, and it was Mum's job to organise them all."

"Let's go down there straight after breakfast," said Kirsty. "I can't wait to see it."

Mr Walker made a yummy breakfast and then the girls walked down to the peace garden. Mrs Walker was already there, and she waved when she saw them.

"I'm glad you're here," she said. "Could you pour some orange juice ready for the visitors?

"We'd love to help," said Kirsty.

The girls went over to the refreshment tent. As they were pouring the drinks,

Rachel pointed out the people who worked in the peace garden.

"That blonde lady is Marnie, the head gardener," she said. "She's going to make sure that the plants stay healthy and keep everything looking beautiful and relaxing."

"Who's the red-headed man she's talking to?" Kirsty asked.

"That's Ned," said Rachel. "He is going to run courses in the peace garden to help people relax. He calls it nature therapy. There will be a herb patch, a fruit orchard and lots of insect habitats."

A grey-haired lady in a tweed suit joined Marnie and Ned.

"That's Erica," said Rachel. "She's in charge of the whole peace garden project."

"Oh, I've run out of juice," Kirsty exclaimed.

She went to open some more, and gasped.

"Rachel, these cartons are glowing," she whispered. "I think we might see some magic today after all."

The girls leaned closer, and the glow grew stronger. Then a tiny, glittering fairy peeped around the corner of a carton. She was wearing a simple jumpsuit and ballet pumps, and there was a garland of flowers in her dark hair.

"Oh my goodness," Rachel whispered. "Hello, what's your name? Welcome to the peace garden."

"Thank you," said the fairy. "I'm Jacinda the Peace Fairy, and my special magic inspires people to do the right thing and help others. I keep the peace here and in Fairyland."

"It's lovely to meet you," said Kirsty. "Have you come to watch the opening ceremony?"

"Yes," said Jacinda, smiling. "I want to give a little magic to the garden, to make sure it is always a calm and healing place."

"What a lovely idea," said Rachel.

Jacinda took a delicate magnifying glass out of her pocket. It had a rim of pure gold, and the handle was encrusted with sparkling gems.

"This is my magnificent magnifying glass," she said. "It makes sure that people see things from each other's point of view. I'm going to use it to cast a spell over the whole garden, so that it will always be a place of peace."

She held up the glass and the sun beamed

through the lens, shining its light across the garden. Jacinda began her spell.

"With this beam of peaceful light
None shall argue, shout or fight.
See the other – oh!"

The magnifying glass was whipped out of her hand. Behind her, a tall figure in a hooded cloak cackled with laughter.

Read Jacinda the Peace Fairy to find out what adventures are in store for Kirsty and Rachel!

Read the brand-new series
from Daisy Meadows...

Ride. Dream. Believe.

Meet best friends Aisha and Emily
and journey to the secret world of
Unicorn Valley!

Calling all parents, carers and teachers!
The Rainbow Magic fairies are here to help
your child enter the magical world of reading.
Whatever reading stage they are at, there's
a Rainbow Magic book for everyone!
Here is Lydia the Reading Fairy's guide to
supporting your child's journey at all levels.

Starting Out

1 Our Rainbow Magic Beginner Readers are perfect for first-time readers who are just beginning to develop reading skills and confidence. Approved by teachers, they contain a full range of educational levelling, as well as lively full-colour illustrations.

Developing Readers

2 Rainbow Magic Early Readers contain longer stories and wider vocabulary for building stamina and growing confidence. These are adaptations of our most popular Rainbow Magic stories, specially developed for younger readers in conjunction with an Early Years reading consultant, with full-colour illustrations.

Going Solo

3 The Rainbow Magic chapter books – a mixture of series and one-off specials – contain accessible writing to encourage your child to venture into reading independently. These highly collectible and much-loved magical stories inspire a love of reading to last a lifetime.

www.rainbowmagicbooks.co.uk

"Rainbow Magic got my daughter reading chapter books. Great sparkly covers, cute fairies and traditional stories full of magic that she found impossible to put down"
- Mother of Edie (6 years)

"Florence LOVES the Rainbow Magic books. She really enjoys reading now"
- Mother of Florence (6 years)

Read along the Reading Rainbow!

Well done – you have completed the book!

This book was worth 2 stars.

See how far you have climbed on the Reading Rainbow opposite.
The more books you read, the more stars you can colour in
and the closer you will be to becoming a Royal Fairy!

Do you want to print your own Reading Rainbow?

1) Go to the Rainbow Magic website

2) Download and print out the poster

3) Colour in a star for every book you finish
and climb the Reading Rainbow

4) For every step up the rainbow,
you can download your very own certificate

There's all this and lots more at
rainbowmagicbooks.co.uk

You'll find activities, stories, a special newsletter
AND you can search for the fairy with your name!